All Yo

Sun Therapy

Vijaya Kumar

New Dawn

NEW DAWN
An imprint of Sterling Publishers (P) Ltd.
L-10, Green Park Extension, New Delhi-110016
Ph.: 6191784, 6191785, 6191023 Fax: 91-11-6190028
E-mail: ghai@nde.vsnl.net.in
Internet: http://www.sterlingpublishers.com

All You Wanted to Know About - Sun Therapy
©2001, Sterling Publishers Private Limited
ISBN 81 207 2368 6

All rights are reserved. No part of this publication may be
reproduced, stored in a retrieval system or transmitted, in any form
or by any means, mechanical, photocopying, recording or
otherwise, without prior written permission of the publisher.

Illustrations by Chokhe Lal

Published by Sterling Publishers Pvt. Ltd., New Delhi-110016.
Lasertypeset by Vikas Compographics, New Delhi-110029.
Printed at Shagun Composer New Delhi-110029.

Contents

Introduction

Sun-rays possess therapeutic powers that are beneficial to one's health, both physical and mental. Growth and development of one's body is dependent on sunlight which consists of energy and colour. Numerous experiments have been conducted to prove that the closer a therapeutic system is to nature, the more powerful and influential it is. Making obeisance to the Sun early in the morning helps to purify and harmonise the functioning of the various organs in the body.

Benefits of Sun Therapy

- Solar power, a natural source of energy, is available free of cost and in abundance.
- Sun-rays have healing powers, and in conjunction with medicines, water, colour, gems, etc., they are even more effective.
- Sunlight converts the inactive Vitamin D in our bodies to its active form, which is essential for healthy bones.
- Solarised water, sugar, oil, etc., are effective in curing ailments.

- Sun-rays are useful in correcting the deficiency or excess of a particular chemical in any part of the body.
- The sun is also a good source for pigmentation of one's skin.
- The early rays of the sun are beneficial in activating the pituitary glands.

Healing with Colours

- Colour therapy, related to solar therapy, is the most natural of all therapeutic medicinal systems.
- Where there is sunlight, there is energy and colour, and hence sun-rays form the basis of colour therapy.
- The various parts of the body as well as the organs are affected by different colours.
- Colour therapy helps in restoring the colour and the chemical balance.

- Like homoeopathy, colour therapy also eliminates the toxins from the body.
- Sunlight, colour and heat affect the development and growth of the body in several ways.
- The coolness or warmth of the various colours can be measured. For example, when you place a thermometer in a glass of water and pass red or blue rays through it, the thermometer will register a rise or fall in temperature, showing heat or coolness, respectively.

- Of the seven colours emitted by the sun — violet, indigo, blue, green, yellow, orange and red — only red, yellow and blue are primary colours. The others are secondary and tertiary colours, which are combinations of these primary colours.
- These seven colours of the sun-rays have therapeutic qualities.
- The seven colours are divided into three groups, and the therapist needs to choose only one group for treatment.
- The rays of any colour can be absorbed by the body with the help of coloured glass.

- Solarisation of water, oil or granulated sugar can be effected by exposing these to the sun in a coloured bottle. Solarisation produces medicinal properties in these substances.
- Colour therapy has been proved to cure even cases of addiction, apart from other diseases.
- The three groups that serve the therapist's purpose are:
  - Red, orange and yellow
  - Green
  - Blue, indigo and violet

Colour-charged Medicines

- Colour-charged medicines come in three varieties — orange-charged, green-charged and blue-charged.
- Solarised water, sugar, sugar pills, and oil or glycerine are some of the medicines that are administered to patients.
- Radiation from the sun's rays, for a specific time-period, helps in correcting the deficiency or excess of any particular colour or chemical that has upset the body's functioning.

Solarised Water

- Fill clean bottles of orange, green and blue colours with drinking water, leaving ¼th of the bottles empty.

- Close these bottles with lids, and keep them in the sun for six to eight hours, ensuring that they are kept apart, so that their shadows do not fall upon each other.

- These bottles now contain solarised water, and this water, which has medicinal power, can be stored and administered for four to five days.

- People above 12 years of age need to take nearly half a cup of the solarised water, while an infant can take one teaspoon; a child aged between 1 - 5 years can take one tablespoon; and children in the age group of 5-12 years can take a quarter cup.
- A person having more than one complaint can take two medicines together.
- Solarised water is better than solarised sugar, though both have the same medicinal value when they are in the same coloured bottles.

Solarised Sugar

- Half fill the orange, blue and green-coloured bottles with granulated sugar.
- Keep them in the sun every day, for a month.
- During the night, keep them with their lids tightly closed, in a safe place.
- Shake them every day, cleaning the outside of the bottles.
- If necessary, the sugar can be used after 15 days.
- These solar-charged bottles of sugar can be kept and used for a long period, provided they are

kept in the sun for four-five days, every two or three months.

- Half a teaspoon of the solarised sugar can be administered to adults.

Solarised Sugar Pills

- Half fill the orange, green and blue-coloured bottles with milk-sugar pills (the ones that are used in homoeopathy).
- Keep them out in the sun every day for three months.
- Allow the sun-rays to fall on them, by rotating the bottles every now and then, so as to allow all the pills to be properly charged.

15

- Shake the bottles gently every day, taking care that the pills do not break.
- Every evening, the bottles should be closed properly, and cleaned from outside.
- Adults can be administered six pills.

Solarised Oil and Glycerine
- Half fill the orange and green-coloured bottles with mustard or sesame oil.
- Half fill the blue bottles with coconut oil or glycerine or ghee (clarified butter).
- Keep all these bottles in the sun for a month, shaking them every

day and cleaning them from outside.

- The bottles are ready for use after a month.
- Once in two-three months, keep them in the sun for four-five days.
- Ensure that the bottles of different colours are not kept close to each other.

Solarised Air
- Keep thoroughly cleaned orange, green and blue-coloured bottles in the sun for five minutes.
- Then tightly close the lids, and store them safely.

- These bottles containing charged air can be used, according to their colour, for asthma patients or for those afflicted with lung problems.

Solar Radiation

- Radiation, like injection, has a direct effect on the functioning of one's body.
- The rays of the sun can remedy any deficiency, excess or imbalance between the colour and chemical composition.
- Radiation can be utilised directly from the sun.

- Depending on the ailment, the patient can choose the requisite colour, and apply oil on the body from an orange or blue-coloured bottle, and then the patient can sunbathe for 15 to 30 minutes.
- People with sensitive skin should take extra care to ensure that they do not get sunburnt.
- During sunbathing, ensure that the afflicted part of the body directly faces the sun so that the sun-rays can be effective.

Solarised Orange Medicines
- Orange-charged medicines are alkaline in effect.

19

- They have a heating and stimulating nature.
- Orange colour affects the abdominal region: stomach, liver, intestines, kidneys and spleen.
- Blood circulation improves greatly after using these medicines.
- Muscles become healthy and toned after using these orange-charged medicines.
- These medicines cure ailments like fever, pneumonia, influenza, cough, tuberculosis, nervous and heart disorders, paralysis, breathing and gas problems, lung troubles, etc.

- They help to build up an appetite, and also assist in digestion.
- They help in weight reduction, remove weakness, and strengthen the mind.
- Dysmenorrhoea or other gynaecological problems are treated with these medicines.
- They should be taken within 15-30 minutes after meals.
- Orange-charged air is specially good for lung-related problems.
- Oil from solarised orange bottles brings relief to joint pains.
- These medicines help in curing bed-wetting, kidney and spleen-

related problems, and in lactation.

Solarised Green Medicines

- As nature's colour, green-charged medicines neutralise one's health problems.
- Being a combination of blue and yellow, the medicines balance the body's chemistry.
- They build and tone up muscles, giving them more energy.
- They purify blood, and help in eliminating foreign bodies from the system.
- The brain and the nerve centres get stimulated.

- The green medicine should be taken on an empty stomach, or one hour before meals.
- Solarised green medicines are beneficial in curing indigestion and stomach-ache, diabetes, gonorrhoea, smallpox, fevers like malaria and typhoid, ulcers, cancer, high blood pressure, boils and pimples, warts, eczema, dry cough, cold and headaches, as well as afflictions of the nervous system, liver, skin, kidneys, eyes, etc.

Solarised Blue Medicines

- Being acidic in effect, blue-charged medicines are cooling and soothing.
- They act as very good antiseptics.
- Blue colour mostly affects the throat and the region above it.
- As these medicines are of a soothing colour, they help in alleviating burning sensations in the body.
- Oedema and swellings caused by wind in the body can be cured by these medicines.
- These medicines are very good for tonsillitis, throat ailments,

toothache and swelling of gums, pyorrhoea and ulcers in the mouth.

- They are good for controlling high blood pressure, hysteria and mental disorders as well as insomnia.
- They are also very effective in curing skin problems.
- Sunstroke, internal haemorrhage, etc., can be cured, because blue has a soothing effect.
- High fever and headaches can be treated with these medicines.
- They cure excessive bleeding during menstruation, and leucorrhoea.

- Excessive thirst, jaundice, food poisoning and poisonous insect bites can be treated with the help of these solarised medicines.
- Epilepsy, vomiting, nausea, cholera, dysentery, diarrhoea, etc., can be cured.
- To find instant relief from burns on any part of the body, pour solarised water or oil from blue-coloured bottles on the affected part, and focus blue rays on it. (Rays can be focussed with the help of a coloured glass.)
- These medicines should normally be taken on an empty

stomach, or one hour before meals.

- Solarised blue air provides relief when there is inflammation of the nose.
- Solarised oil from a blue-coloured bottle helps in bringing down high fever.

Treatment of Diseases

Abdominal Gas
- Abdominal gas may lead to constipation, chest pain and giddiness.
- Solarised green water and solarised orange water should be taken twice or thrice a day.

Abdominal Pain
- Rubbing solarised blue oil and focussing blue rays on the lower abdomen help in easing abdominal pain.

Anaemia

- Solarised orange water and solarised green water, both help in strengthening one's body during convalescence.

- They also help in stimulating the circulatory system, and in producing more red blood cells in the body.

Baldness

- Rubbing solarised blue oil on the scalp twice a day, and then focussing blue rays on the affected area will arrest falling of hair and premature greying, as well as help in removing dandruff. (This should be continued for a long period for best results.)

Bed-wetting

- Take solarised orange medicine thrice a day.
- At bedtime, take a dose of solarised orange sugar.

Blood Pressure

- Take solarised green water and solarised blue water for high blood pressure.
- If you have low blood pressure, then take solarised green water and solarised orange water twice or thrice daily.

Breathing Problems

- Breathing problems can be cured if solarised orange water is taken twice a day.
- If congestion causes trouble in breathing, a dose of solarised green medicine is recommended. This should be followed by massaging the chest and the back with solarised orange oil.
- When phlegm aggravates the breathing problem, radiation from orange rays helps in easing the problem.

Burns

- Application of solarised blue oil and blue radiation over the burnt part bring quick relief.
- Drink solarised green water.

Cholera

- Give two to three doses of solarised blue water every hour, for relieving watery motions and vomiting.
- When some relief is felt, give a mixture of solarised green and orange medicines.
- For complete relief, expose the patient to the radiation of blue rays for 15 minutes at regular intervals for a few days.

Chickenpox or Smallpox

- Mix together three parts of solarised green water with one part of solarised white water, and take it twice a day.
- One cup of solarised green water in the morning is also beneficial.
- Rubbing solarised blue oil on the forehead will bring down high fever.
- Radiation of blue rays on the itchy spots for ten minutes gives a soothing effect.

34

Cold and Cough
- Solarised green water is ideal for cold and cough.
- Take solarised orange medicine twice a day, and solarised green medicine once in the morning for a running nose.

Constipation
- A cup of solarised green water in the morning, and a cup of solarised orange water after meals twice a day helps in curing severe constipation.

Diabetes

- Every day, administer three doses of solarised green water.

- During hot weather, give a mixture of equal parts of solarised green water and solarised blue water.

- During cold weather, use solarised orange and solarised green water.

Diarrhoea

- Take solarised green water, frequently alternating it with solarised blue water.

Dysentery

- Take solarised blue water and solarised green water alternately.
- Expose to the radiation of blue rays for 15 minutes twice a day.

Ear Problems

- Use warm solarised blue oil as ear drops twice a day to treat boils in the ear.
- Two drops of solarised green or solarised orange oil helps in relieving ear pain.
- Two drops of solarised blue glycerine, thrice a day, controls discharge from the ear.
- Use of red rays inside and around the ears for 10 minutes daily will help one whose hearing is affected.

Eye Problems

- For watering, redness, itching and pain in the eyes, wash the eyes with solarised green water frequently.
- Administer the solarised green water as eye drops twice or thrice a day.
- Expose to the radiation of blue rays for three minutes.

Fever

- Treat high fever by exposing the head to the radiation of blue rays for 10 minutes, every half an hour.
- Once the temperature comes down, take solarised green water thrice a day before meals.
- For malarial high fever, take solarised blue water twice or thrice a day.

- For fevers accompanied by headaches, rub solarised blue oil on the forehead.
- For excessive phlegm, massage the chest with solarised orange oil.
- For chest congestion caused by pneumonia, influenza, etc., give solarised green water and solarised orange water.

Gonorrhoea

- Give two or three doses of solarised green and solarised blue water.

- Lightly massage the lower abdomen and genitals with solarised blue oil.

- In case of swelling and pus, expose to the radiation of blue rays for 15 minutes.

Gynaecological Problems

- Excessive bleeding that lasts for a long period should be treated with a mixture of two parts of solarised blue water and one part of solarised green water. This is to be taken thrice before meals daily.
- The abdomen should be massaged with solarised blue oil.
- Excessive pain that accompanies scanty bleeding can be cured by taking two parts of solarised orange, and one part of solarised green medicines.

43

- This should be followed by massaging the lower abdomen with solarised orange oil.

Headache
- Headaches caused by fever should be treated by rubbing solarised green or solarised blue oil on the forehead.
- Expose to the radiation of blue rays for 10 minutes.
- Headache during menstruation can be· relieved by applying solarised blue oil on the forehead.

- For supplementary effect, expose to the radiation of blue rays.

Heart Problems
- To cure pain in the heart region, or to treat palpitation, take one dose of solarised green water and two doses of solarised orange water daily.
- The problem of high cholesterol can be treated by exposing the chest to the radiation of yellow rays.

Hysteria
- Take solarised blue medicine daily.
- The head should be exposed to the radiation of blue rays.

- Apply solarised blue oil on the head.
- Wear blue clothes while in the sunlight.

Inflammation

- Solarised blue oil should be applied on the inflamed area.
- Expose the affected area to the radiation of blue rays.
- Solarised orange oil should be applied on the inflamed area, if the inflammation is due to cold weather.
- In such a case, solarised green water may also be taken.

Insect Bite

- Massaging solarised blue oil gives instant relief from any insect bite.

Insomnia

- Massage the head with solarised blue oil.
- At bedtime, take a dose of solarised blue sugar.

Jaundice

- Mix two parts of solarised blue water with one part of solarised green water, and take it as recommended.
- In acute cases, solarised green medicine will help.

Kidney Problems

- The problem of kidney stones can be cured by taking one dose of solarised green and two doses of solarised orange water twice a day.
- Exposing to the radiation of orange rays for 15 minutes also helps.

Leucorrhoea

- Take a mixture of two parts of solarised blue water and one part of solarised green water thrice a day.
- Solarised blue water can be used as a vaginal douche, twice a day.

48

Liver Problems

- Take a dose of solarised green water in the morning, in case of poor digestion or a sluggish liver.
- Take solarised orange water twice a day after meals.
- Take yellow ray radiation on the stomach twice a day for 15 minutes each time.
- For an enlarged liver, take solarised green water thrice a day.
- Also, apply solarised blue oil on the abdominal region.

Lung Problems

- If tuberculosis is suspected, or if there is phlegm in the lungs, or even to cure pneumonia, take solarised green water and solarised orange water.
- Rub solarised orange oil on the chest.
- Take yellow ray radiation.

Mental Disorders

- For all symptoms of psychotic conditions, insomnia, phobias, restlessness, headaches and dizziness, lack of concentration and appetite, massage solarised blue oil on the scalp for 10 minutes.
- After meals (breakfast and lunch), exposure to radiation of blue rays in mild sunlight is recommended.
- Wear blue clothes while in the sunshine.

Migraine

- Take solarised green water and solarised orange water frequently.
- Lightly massage the forehead with solarised green oil.

Mumps

- Drink solarised green water twice a day.
- Apply solarised blue oil on the throat.

Mouth Problems

- Rinse your mouth with solarised blue water for relief from blisters in the mouth, bleeding and inflamed gums, toothache, pyorrhoea, etc.

- Paint the blisters or gums with solarised blue glycerine.

- Drink two or three doses of solarised green water.

Nausea

- Take two or three doses of solarised blue water if the nausea is due to bile.
- If it is due to indigestion, take solarised green water and solarised orange water.

Nose Bleed

- Mix two parts of solarised blue water and one part of solarised green water, and drink two doses of this concoction.
- Rub solarised blue oil on the head and the forehead.
- Take blue ray radiations.

Obesity

- Drink a cup of solarised green water in the morning on an empty stomach.
- Drink half a cup of solarised orange water twice a day after meals.
- Take red ray radiation on the bare body for 10 minutes, followed by white ray radiation for five minutes. Repeat this process, and follow this routine every day for 40 days regularly, at a specific time.

Pain in the Joints

- Solarised orange oil helps in relieving pain in the joints, if taken twice or thrice a day.

Paralysis

- One cup of solarised green water on an empty stomach in the morning should be given to a patient who has had a stroke.
- Twice a day, give him/her solarised orange medicine.
- Massage the paralysed limbs with solarised orange oil.
- Give orange ray radiation twice or thrice a day.

Piles

- Drink solarised green water two-three times a day, to cure pain or itching at or near the anus.
- Apply solarised green oil or solarised blue oil on it and inside it.
- For bleeding piles, use solarised blue water twice or thrice a day.

Sciatica

- Drink a mixture of equal parts of solarised green water and solarised orange water thrice a day.
- Massage the leg with solarised orange oil.
- Take orange ray radiation.

57

Skin Problems

- Drink two-three doses of solarised green water for itching of the skin, boils, urticaria, eczema, ringworm, white patches, etc.
- Apply solarised blue oil on the affected area of the skin for quick relief.
- Solarised blue oil is also beneficial for boils where the skin reddens and pain sets in.
- If the boil is in the bursting stage, apply solarised orange oil, and drink solarised green water three to four times a day.

Spleen Problems

- Drink one dose of solarised green water, and two doses of solarised orange water daily, for an enlarged spleen.
- Externally apply solarised orange oil on the spleen area.
- Yellow ray radiation should also be taken.

Stomach Problems

- Drink two or three doses of solarised orange water for stomach-ache or flatulence.

Sunstroke

- Drink solarised blue water.
- Gargle with solarised blue water.
- Take blue ray radiation on your back.

Syphilis

- Drink solarised green water thrice a day.
- Apply solarised blue oil all over the body.
- Take blue ray radiation.

Throat Problems

- Gargle with solarised blue water for septic tonsils.
- Drink solarised green water.
- Paint the tonsils with solarised blue glycerine.

Typhoid

- Drink solarised green water to bring down low-grade fever.
- If the fever is accompanied by diarrhoea, take blue ray radiation on the abdomen.
- For very high fever, drink solarised blue water thrice a day, and take blue ray radiation on the spine for 15 minutes.

Ulcers

- One dose of solarised green water and two doses of solarised blue water before meals will relieve one of ulcers.
- Blue ray radiation on the stomach for 15 minutes, twice a day, is beneficial.

Whooping Cough

- Drink solarised green water.
- Gargle with solarised blue water.

Wounds

- Wash the wound with solarised blue water.
- Apply solarised blue oil on it for quick healing.

Benefits of Surya Namaskar

- Regular practice of Surya Namaskar enables you to experience the truth that the sun is the source of energy for all that exists.
- Regular practice helps you to achieve good health, and a greater balance of mind, and also helps you conquer inertia and fatigue.
- Like all yogic asanas, Surya Namaskar purifies and

harmonises the various organs of the body.

- They stimulate and tone up all the nerve centres.
- They help in controlling the secretions of the ductless glands.
- They also help in energising the brain cells.
- They help in tuning the capacity of the body to receive and utilise cosmic energy.
- One can experience vitality, beauty, joy and harmony, if one spends fifteen to twenty minutes every day doing Surya Namaskar.

- Through the daily practice of Surya Namaskar, you will find that your relationships with others will improve.
- You will feel one with all that is around you, as your tensions and stresses melt away, and conflicts and doubts disappear.
- You will gradually realise that memory or attachment to the past or future is false, hollow and impermanent.
- With this realisation, you are released from all tensions and conflicts, leading you to a feeling of being truly free.

- Surya Namaskar does not belong to any religion, but it has in it a profound spiritual content, that takes you to new and powerful parameters of awareness.
- Surya Namaskar exercises and tones up the muscles, the bones, the various systems, the glands and the organs of the body.
- It also energises the energy centres of the body.
- You become mentally alert as well as physically fit, and start feeling one with nature.

- These exercises cleanse not only your body, but also your mind and intellect.
- It is best to do them early in the morning.

Mantras

- Mantras are an essential part of Surya Namaskar.
- A mantra is an energised sound.
- These energised sounds and vibrations create the energy that one seeks.
- The chanting of mantras in the proper manner can energise and sensitise the human mind, making it alert and watchful, and thus making it fit to receive energy.

- While chanting the mantras, the focus should be on the sounds, and the meaning of the sounds, if possible.
- If used properly, a mantra can liberate you, and allow you to experience bliss.
- A mantra can calm an agitated mind, if it is properly received with reverence and used correctly.
- Mantras are essential for exercising and disciplining the mind.
- A mantra, if properly pronounced, can connect you

69

with the joyful, blissful cosmic energies and vital forces that sustain all creation.

- It can lift you from the mundane life to experience the joy, harmony and beauty of existence.
- The mantras should be chanted loudly and rhythmically.
- The *beeja* or seed mantra *Aum* is the most important one.
- "Aum" stands for A — Vishnu, U — Shiva, and M — Brahma: preserving, destroying and creating, respectively.
- The beeja mantras used during the Surya Namaskar are:

Aum Hram

Aum Hreem

Aum Hroom

Aum Hraim

Aum Hraum

Aum Hrāh

- The twelve mantras are as follows:

Aum Hram Mitrāiya Namah

ॐ हरम् मित्राय नमः

Aum Hreem Ravayé Namah

ॐ हरीम् रवये नमः

Aum Hroom Suryāya Namah

ॐ हरूम् सूर्याय नमः

Aum Hraim Bhanāvé Namah

ॐ हरैम् भानवे नमः

71

Aum Hraum Khagāya Namah

ॐ हरौम् खगाय नमः

Aum Hrāh Pushné Namah

ॐ हराह पुश्ने नमः

Aum Hram Hiranyagarbhāya Namah

ॐ हरम् हिरण्यगर्भाय नमः

Aum Hreem Mareechayé Namah

ॐ हरीम् मरीचये नमः

Aum Hroom Ādityāya Namah

ॐ हरूम् आदित्याय नमः

Aum Hraim Sāvitré Namah

ॐ हरैम् सावित्रे नमः

Aum Hraum Arkāya Namah

ॐ हरौम् अर्काय नमः

Aum Hrāh Bhāskarāya Namah

ॐ हराह भास्कराय नमः

72

- Each step of the Surya Namaskar is to be followed by loud chanting of one of the mantras.
- The names of the Sun, along with their meanings, are as follows:

Mitra	—	friend
Ravi	—	shining
Surya	—	beautiful light
Bhānu	—	brilliant
Khaga	—	one who moves in the sky
Pushān	—	giver of strength
Hiranya-garbha	—	golden-centred
Mareechi	—	lord of dawn
Āditya	—	son of Aditi

Sāvitr	—	beneficent
Arka	—	energy
Bhāskara	—	leading to enlightenment

- Before taking up each position of the Surya Namaskar, say loudly and clearly one of the names of the sun, along with the beeja mantra (the seed or basic mantra) and the *pranava* (the life force or vital breath), eg,
  Aum Hram Mitrāiya Namah
- The vibrations set off by the chanting of mantras reach every cell in the body, and you experience energy flowing into your whole being.

74

- Mantra, also known as *prāna* (life-breath) and *shabda* (verbal articulation of sound) is the fusion of *prāna* and *shabda* which harmonises the mind-energy, leading to awareness and alertness.
- These mantras are beneficent and joyous ones.
- For chanting these mantras and practising the Surya Namaskar, you must exercise control over your food intake, eating only what the body requires. Your actions and habits must be regulated, with a fixed schedule

for eating, sleeping and exercising; your clothing should be clean and loose; and your thoughts should be clean and positive.

Surya Namaskar

First Step

- Stand straight, facing the sun.
- Keep your heels and toes together, and the knees and back straight.
- Join your hands together, with palms touching each other in the form of 'Namaskar'.
- Take a deep breath through the nose keeping the mouth closed, filling the lungs with air.
- Chant the first mantra,
  Aum Hram Mitrāiya Namah,
  loudly and clearly, and exhale.

- Then again fill your lungs with a deep breath, and slowly raise both your hands above your head and then behind, keeping the arms straight.
- At the same time, raise your head up and tilt it backwards.

Figure 1

Second Step

- While exhaling slowly, bend down till the palms touch the ground beside the legs.
- The distance between the palms should equal the length of your arm from the elbow to the fingertips.
- The fingers should be straight, the arms should bend only at the wrist, and the knees should be together and straight.
- The nose and forehead should touch the knees.
- Chant the next mantra, *Aum Hreem Ravayé Namah,*

loudly and clearly, after taking a deep breath, and exhale as you chant.

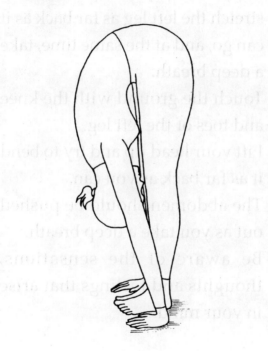

Figure 2

Third Step

- Sit on your right foot, body supported by the palms, and stretch the left leg as far back as it can go, and at the same time, take a deep breath.

- Touch the ground with the knee and toes of the left leg.

- Lift your head up and try to bend it as far back as you can.

- The abdomen should be pushed out as you take a deep breath.

- Be aware of the sensations, thoughts and feelings that arise in your mind.

- Chant the mantra,
  Aum Hroom Suryāya Namah,
  as you exhale.

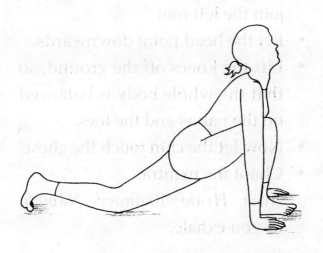

Figure 3

Fourth Step

- Take a deep breath, and keeping the body balanced on the palms, move the right foot backwards to join the left foot.
- Let the head point downwards.
- Lift the knees off the ground, so that the whole body is balanced on the palms and the toes.
- Now let the chin touch the chest.
- Chant the mantra, *Aum Hram Bhānavé Namah*, as you exhale.

Figure 4

Fifth Step

- With palms still on the ground, bend your arms, and let the body touch the ground with the toes, knees, chest and forehead, taking a deep breath at the same time.

- While exhaling, pull your abdomen in, making sure that it does not touch the ground, but see that the nose touches the ground.

- Take a deep breath, and then chant the mantra, *Aum Hraum Khagāya Namah*, as you exhale.

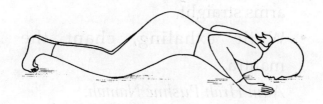

Figure 5

Sixth Step

- Take a deep breath, and with the palms still on the ground, lift your head and chest off the ground.
- Bend your upper body as far back as you can, keeping the arms straight.
- While exhaling, chant the mantra,
  Aum Hrāh Pushné Namah.

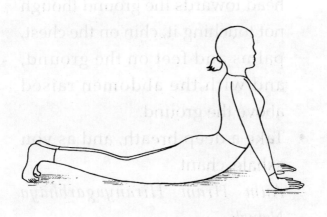

Figure 6

Seventh Step

- Take a deep breath, and while exhaling, come back to the position of the fourth step, ie, head towards the ground though not touching it, chin on the chest, palms and feet on the ground, and with the abdomen raised above the ground.

- Take a deep breath, and as you exhale, chant
Aum Hram Hiranyagarbhāya Namah.

Eighth Step

- Taking a deep breath, bring the right leg forward and bend it at the knee so that it is between the palms, with the foot flat on the ground.
- This position is the same as in the third step.
- As you exhale, chant *Aum Hreem Mareechayé Namah*.

Ninth Step

- As you inhale, bring the left leg also forward, so that both the feet rest between the palms.
- Allow the forehead and the nose to touch the front of the knees after you straighten up your legs (similar to the second step).
- As you exhale, chant *Aum Hroom Ādityāya Namah*.

Tenth Step

- As you inhale, raise your palms from the ground, straighten the back, and take the hands above your head.
- Holding the arms straight, bend them backwards behind the head.
- At the same time, lift your head and bend it backwards.
- As you exhale, chant
  Aum Hraim Sāvitré Namah.

Eleventh Step

- Lower the hands and head, and bring the palms together as in the first step.
- Take a deep breath, and as you exhale, chant *Aum Hraum Arkāya Namah.*

Twelfth Step

- Move the hands to the sides of the body.
- Take a deep breath, and as you exhale, chant
  Aum Hrāḥ Bhāskarāya Namah.

Yoga and Body Postures

- Surya Namaskar, supplemented with yoga, enables the body to be united with the mind, the matter with the spirit, and the physical with the spiritual.
- Through regular practice of Surya Namaskar, and yoga, one can transcend the mundane world, and attain the state of higher consciousness.
- Surya Namaskar, accompanied by yoga asanas, will lead to the union of the self with the Divine Being.

- Yoga, a way of life with a distinct philosophy, stresses on a code of ethics that is based on the basic and universal principles of truth, non-violence and moderation.
- By regularly practising yoga, you will achieve purity, contentment, self-awareness, and the will to surrender to the will of God.
- Yoga asanas energise the central nervous system.
- All the organs and systems in the body get rejuvenated, thus complementing the beneficial effects of sun therapy.

Padahastasana

- Stand erect with legs together, hands by the sides of the thighs, gaze in front.
- Slowly bend forward, as much as possible.
- As you are bending, try to place the palms, with fingers pointing forward, on the ground, on either side of the legs.
- Place the forehead between the knees.
- After five breaths, return to the original position.

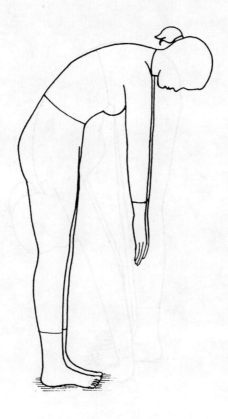

Padahastasana (a)

99

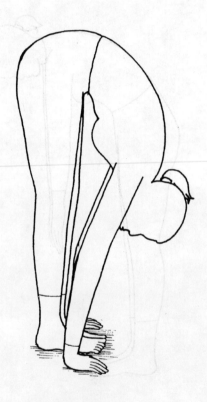

Padahastasana (b)

100

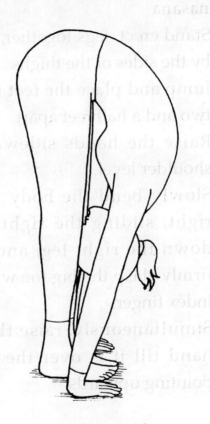

Padahastasana (c)

101

Konasana

- Stand erect, legs together, hands by the sides of the thighs.
- Jump and place the feet two or two and a half feet apart.
- Raise the hands sideways to shoulder level.
- Slowly bend the body to the right, sliding the right hand down the right leg, and then firmly clasp the big toe with the index finger.
- Simultaneously, raise the left hand till it is over the head, pointing upwards.

- Turn your gaze to the fingers of the left hand, and hold this position for a count of five breaths.
- Slowly return to the second position.
- Now repeat this procedure on the left side.
- Return to the first position.

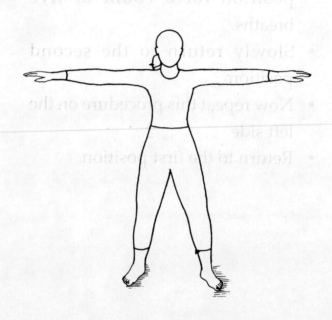

Konasana (a)

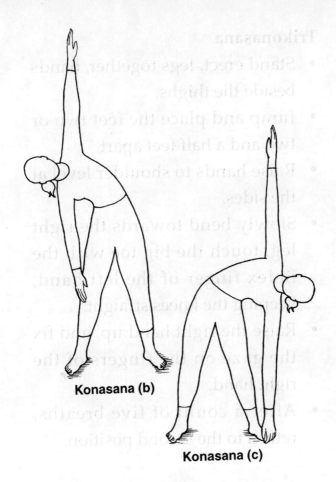

Konasana (b)

Konasana (c)

Trikonasana

- Stand erect, legs together, hands beside the thighs.
- Jump and place the feet two or two and a half feet apart.
- Raise hands to shoulder level at the sides.
- Slowly bend towards the right leg, touch the big toe with the index finger of the left hand, keeping the knees straight.
- Raise the right hand up, and fix the gaze on the fingers of the right hand.
- After a count of five breaths, return to the second position.

- Repeat the procedure on the left side.
- Return to the first position.

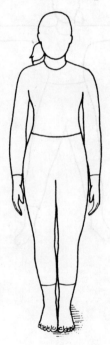

Trikonasana (a)

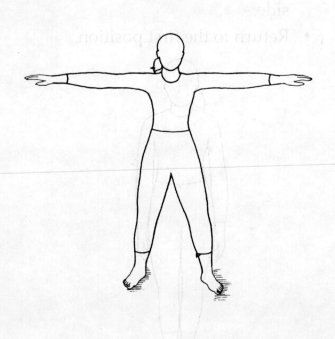

Trikonasana (b)

Trikonasana (c)

Bhujangasana

- Lie face down, with your forehead touching the ground, feet and toes straight along the ground and hands at your sides.
- Lift the upper part of your body and balance the body weight on your palms — as shown in the figure.
- Slowly tilt your head and neck as far back as possible.
- Stay in this position as long as you can, and then come back to the original position.
- This restores your youth and vitality.

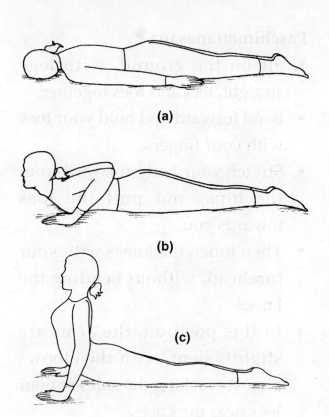

(a)

(b)

(c)

Bhujangasana (a, b and c)

Paschimottanasana

- Sit on the ground, with legs straight, feet and toes together.
- Bend forward and hold your toes with your fingers.
- Stretch your body forward from the hips, and pull the toes towards you.
- Then touch the knees with your forehead, without bending the knees.
- In this position, the arms are slightly bent, with the elbows almost touching the sides of your legs near the knees.

- Stay in this position for three minutes and return to the original position.
- This helps in digestion, and stimulates the kidney, liver and spleen.

Paschimottanasana (a)

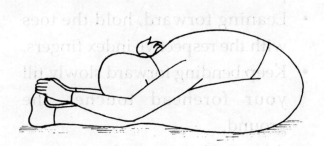

Paschimottanasana (b)

115

Ugrasana

- Sit with both legs stretched out in front.
- Spread out both legs sideways as far away from the body as possible.
- Leaning forward, hold the toes with the respective index fingers.
- Keep bending forward slowly till your forehead touches the ground.
- After maintaining this posture for five breaths, raise the head, release the toes, and return to the original position.

Ugrasana (a and b)

117

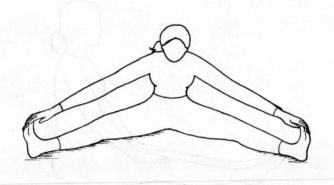

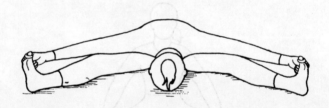

Ugrasana (c and d)

118

Bhadrasana

- Sit with legs stretched out together in front, hands by the sides, palms resting on the ground, fingers pointing forward.
- Fold legs at the knees, and bring together the soles, so that they touch each other.
- Hold legs at the ankle.
- Slowly pull the feet towards the crotch as much as possible, being careful to ensure that the knees remain on the ground, and the body is erect.

- While returning to the original position, loosen the legs, and then assume the first posture.

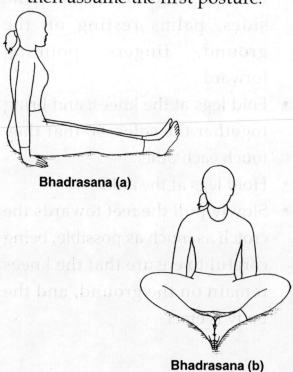

Bhadrasana (a)

Bhadrasana (b)

120

Bhadrasana (c)

Bhadrasana (d)

121

Vajrasana

- This pose is especially beneficial to women.
- Sit with legs stretched out in front, hands by the sides of the body, palms on the ground, fingers pointing forward.
- Fold the right leg at the knee, and place the foot under the right buttock, and likewise with the left foot.
- Place your hands on your thighs.
- Bend forward so that your forehead touches the ground.

- Now extend the arms above the head and remain in this position for two or three minutes.
- Return to resting on the heels and bring your hands to rest near your toes.
- Throw your head back, with the chin pointing towards the ceiling.
- Stay like this for two-three minutes, breathing gently, then return to the original position.
- This asana helps in good bowel movement.

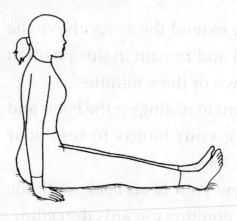

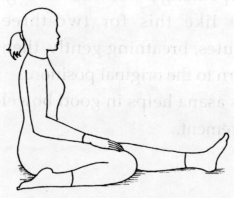

Vajrasana (a and b)

Vajrasana (c)

125

Sarvangasana

- This asana brings vitality and energy to the whole body.
- Lie on the ground on your back, with arms by your sides, legs straight, and toes stretched out.
- Slowly lift both your legs together till they make an angle of 90 degrees with the body.
- Breathe gently in a relaxed manner.
- Then slowly move your legs backwards towards your head.
- At the same time, lift your trunk (or torso) from the ground, so that only your shoulder, neck and head touch the ground.

126

- Now bring the palms to support your trunk by placing them on the hips.
- Then, straighten your arms and let the palms touch your thighs. In this pose your chin rests on your chest.
- Keep breathing gently, while you stay in this asana for half a minute.
- Bring the trunk down to the ground very slowly, till the legs are straight up, with the arms at the sides.
- Then lower the legs to the ground slowly.

- This asana tones up the muscles, eyes, ears, sinuses, ductless glands, kidneys, liver and spleen; clears the throat; and increases the power of concentration.

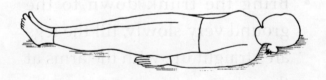

Sarvangasana (a)

Sarvangasana (b)

129

Sarvangasana (c)

130

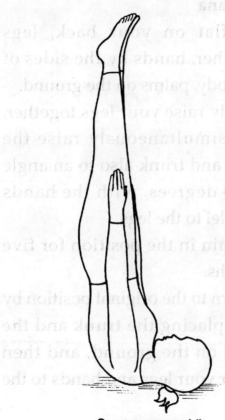

Sarvangasana (d)

Naukasana

- Lie flat on your back, legs together, hands by the sides of the body, palms on the ground.
- Slowly raise your legs together, and simultaneously raise the head and trunk also to an angle of 45 degrees, with the hands parallel to the legs.
- Remain in the position for five breaths.
- Return to the original position by first placing the trunk and the head on the ground, and then lower your legs and hands to the floor.

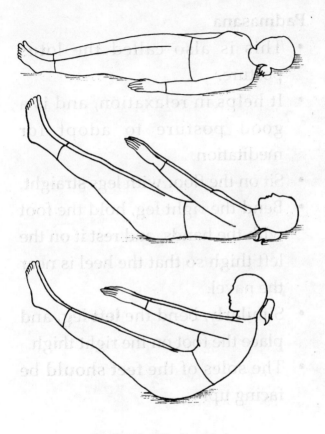

Naukasana (a, b and c)

133

Padmasana

- This is also called the lotus posture.
- It helps in relaxation, and is a good posture to adopt for meditation.
- Sit on the floor with legs straight.
- Bend the right leg, hold the foot with the hands, and rest it on the left thigh so that the heel is near the navel.
- Similarly, bend the left leg, and place the foot on the right thigh.
- The soles of the feet should be facing up.

- Keep the spine erect, place the hands either on the knees, or in the middle where the feet cross each other, with one palm resting upon the other.
- This cures stiffness in the knees and ankles.
- It tones up the abdomen, spine and the abdominal organs.

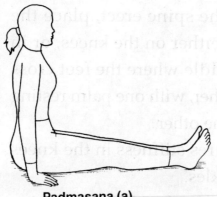

Padmasana (a)

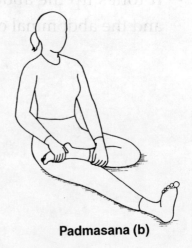

Padmasana (b)

Padmasana (c)

137

Yogamudra

- Sit in Padmasana.
- Taking your hands to the back, hold the wrist of one hand with the other hand, keeping neck and back straight.
- Slowly start bending from your waist. Continue bending till the forehead touches the ground.
- After five breaths, raise your forehead and chest till the back is straight, and slowly releasing the hands, sit erect.

Yogamudra (a)

Yogamudra (b)

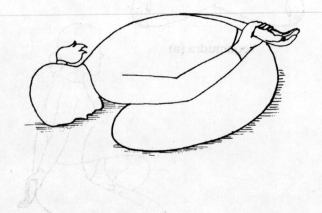

Yogamudra (c)

140

Shavasana

- Lie flat on the ground on your back, in a relaxed pose.
- Close your eyes, and let all the parts of the body relax.
- Breathe gently and observe your breath.
- Shift your attention to the toes, and observe them.
- Gradually, shift your attention to your feet, and observe them.

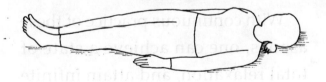

Shavasana

141

- In this manner, observe each part of your body.
- Then concentrate on the seven chakras, starting from the crown to the root chakras. (The chakras comprise: crown; third eye — between the eyebrows; throat; heart; solar plexus; hara — the abdomen; and the root)
- You will experience total relaxation.
- Remain in this position for at least five minutes.

With continuous practice of these asanas, one can achieve a state of total relaxation, and attain infinite energy and joy.

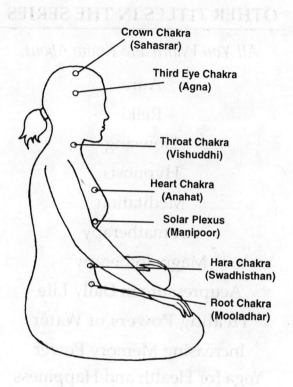

Crown Chakra
(Sahasrar)

Third Eye Chakra
(Agna)

Throat Chakra
(Vishuddhi)

Heart Chakra
(Anahat)

Solar Plexus
(Manipoor)

Hara Chakra
(Swadhisthan)

Root Chakra
(Mooladhar)

Centres of Energy (The Chakras)

OTHER TITLES IN THE SERIES

All You Wanted to Know About

Aura

Reiki

Dowsing

Hypnosis

Meditation

Aromatherapy

Magnetotherapy

Acupressure in Daily Life

Healing Powers of Water

Increasing Memory Power

Yoga for Health and Happiness